roar!

roar!

roar!

roar!

roar!

roar!

roar!

To Maurice —S.R.

ISBN 978-0-06-268007-5

The artist used pen & ink and watercolor to create the illustrations for this book.
Typography by Dana Fritts
19 20 21 22 23 SCP 10 9 8 7 6 5 4 3 2 1

First Edition

ROAR
Like a Dandelion

Words by **Ruth Krauss**

Drawings by **Sergio Ruzzier**

HARPER

An Imprint of HarperCollinsPublishers

Act like a sprinkler in summer

Butt like a billy goat

C row like a rooster, make the sun come up

Dance with a leaf

E at all the locks off the doors

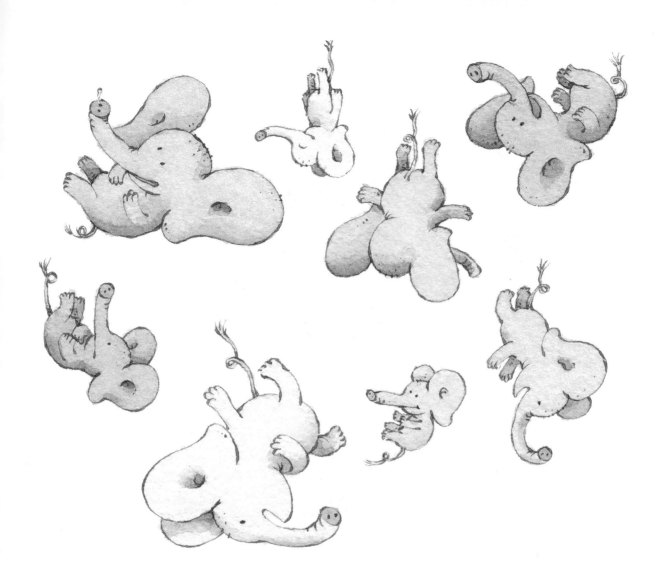

Fall like rain

Go like a road

Hold your arms out
like a little pine tree

I gnore yourself and get mad

Jump like a raindrop

Kick away the snow
and make spring come

Look under the bed for poetry

Make music

Nod YES

Open your eyes, see the sea
Shut them fast, lock it in

Paint a picture of a cage
with an open door
and wait

Quack by a waterfall
and make a pretty rhythm

Roar like a dandelion

Sit in the sun
and shine

Try to hug yourself
in a puddle

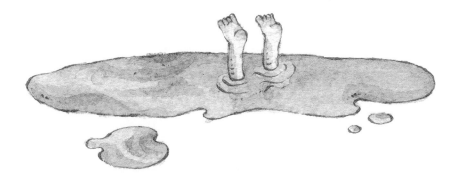

Undress to match
trees in winter

Vote for yourself

W alk backward all the way home

X out all the bad stuff

Yell, "Good morning, big fat world!"

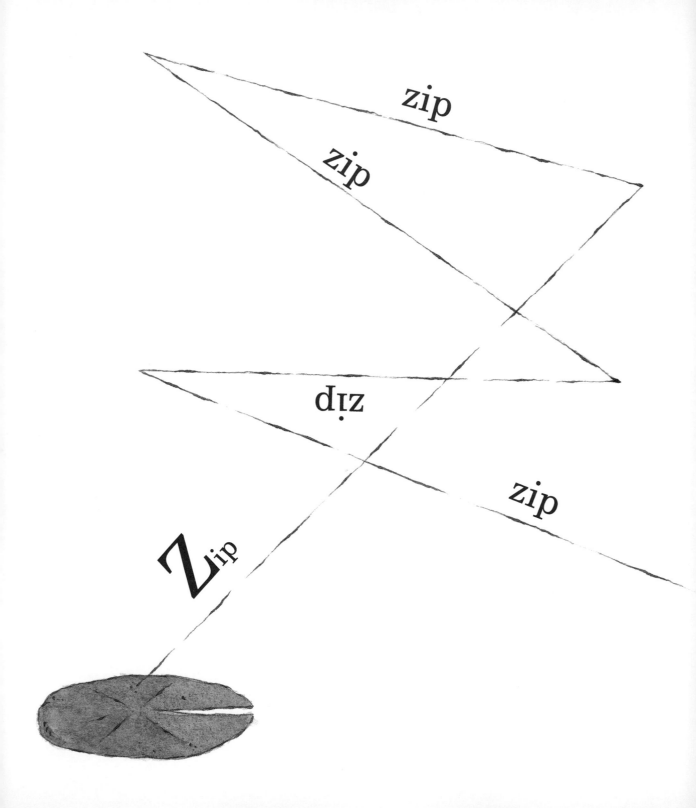

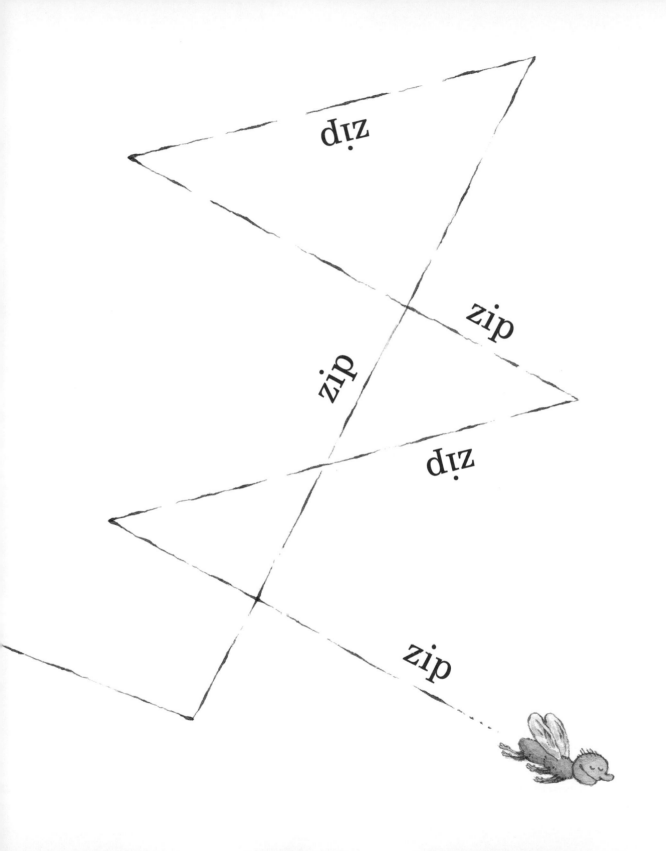